School of Fish
Crossing the Current

By Jane Yolen

Illustrated by Mike Moran

Ready-to-Read

Simon Spotlight
New York   London   Toronto   Sydney   New Delhi

SIMON SPOTLIGHT
An imprint of Simon & Schuster Children's Publishing Division
1230 Avenue of the Americas, New York, New York 10020
This Simon Spotlight edition December 2020
Text copyright © 2020 by Jane Yolen
Illustrations copyright © 2020 by Mike Moran
For information about special discounts for bulk purchases, please contact
Simon & Schuster Special Sales at 1-866-506-1949 or business@simonandschuster.com.
Manufactured in the United States of America 1020 LAK
10 9 8 7 6 5 4 3 2 1
Library of Congress Cataloging-in-Publication Data
Names: Yolen, Jane, author. | Moran, Mike, 1957– illustrator.
Title: Crossing the current / by Jane Yolen ; illustrated by Mike Moran.
Description: Simon Spotlight edition. | New York : Simon Spotlight, 2020.
Series: School of fish | Summary: After saving a little crab from being hit by the shark
bus, a young fish is proclaimed a hero and becomes an assistant crossing guard.
Identifiers: LCCN 2020022739 (print) | LCCN 2020022740 (eBook)
ISBN 9781534466289 (paperback) | ISBN 9781534466296 (hardcover)
ISBN 9781534466302 (eBook)
Subjects: CYAC: Stories in rhyme. | School crossing guards—Fiction.
Schools—Fiction. | Fishes—Fiction. | Marine animals—Fiction.
Classification: LCC PZ8.3.Y76 Ct 2020 (print) | LCC PZ8.3.Y76 (eBook)
DDC [E]—dc23 | LC record available at https://lccn.loc.gov/2020022739

I'm silver. I'm cool.

I'm off to school.

My lunch box is packed,
and that is a fact!

Facts really aren't
a mystery.

We learn them in classes
like science and history.

The shark bus whips
along a tide.

And as we wait
for our school ride,
a little crab
looks left, not right.
He hasn't got the bus
in sight.
WATCH OUT!

Before I think,
before I pause,
I lean right out
and grab his claws.

I pull him back.
He's quite all right,
but both of us
have had a fright.
And that's a FACT!

I tell the crab,
"Close your eyes,
and then
take a deep breath.
Count to ten."

And as he does it,
I do too,
for I am shaking
through and through.
And that's a fact too!

Our count works fine.
There's no more fuss.
He scuttles to
the back of the bus.

Around the school,
the story speeds
of how I had done
a dozen good deeds.

Like ignoring bait,
standing up to a shark
in the bright daylight
(instead of the dark).

Then I am called in
by Principal Pike.
"I have a special job
I think you'll like."

He puts a medal
around my neck.
"Assistant crossing guard.
Correct?"

It's quite an honor.
This I know.
I really should
just go with the flow.

But deep inside, I whimper,
"No! No! No!
I'm not a hero, not a guard.
That job is going
to be too hard."

But out we go
to meet the guard—
a barracuda
in the yard.

He's big and heavy.

I'm little, light.

He could eat me

in a single bite.

Principal Pike talks
of my mighty deed.
It's the last thing
that I need.

I want to dive or swim away.

The barracuda's eyes say

STAY.

So I do.

And that's a fact too.

I close my eyes,
count to ten,
and then I'm ready
once again.

We hold up signs.

We help fish cross.

We save a minnow
who is lost.

We tell the shark bus,
"It's all clear."

We put away
our crossing gear.
It wasn't as bad
as I had feared.

I get to take
my medal home,
polished by the
passing foam.

I sleep with it close,
but not on my neck,
and dream of saving
fish from a wreck.

And in the morning
back at school,
I help fish cross—
and feel *real* cool.